Batter Up!

CHARACTERS

Tommy Time
a boy of today

Carla
a girl of today

Tammy Time
a girl of today

Babe Ruth
superstar baseball player of the past

Lou Gehrig
Babe's teammate

Joe Van Horn
Terry's manager

Terry Fox
superstar baseball player of today

Luis Garcia
Terry's teammate

Johnny Sula
Terry's teammate

SETTING

Today; 1927

Tommy: Go, Carla! Awesome home run!

Carla: I love the sound of a bat smacking a ball.

Tammy: Your hitting won the game for us again. You're going to be the next Terry Fox!

Carla: You think so? Terry Fox is the best home-run hitter ever!

Tommy: Our grandpa says Babe Ruth was the best.

Carla: Babe Ruth? I've heard of him.

Tammy: He was the greatest in the 1920s.

Tommy: In 1921, he hit fifty-nine home runs. That was more than some teams hit the whole year!

Carla: Everyone says Terry Fox might hit eighty home runs this year. I'll bet Babe Ruth couldn't do that.

Tommy: I bet he could!

Carla: Could not!

Tommy: Could too!

Tammy: Let's use our *When Machine* to go back in time and meet Babe Ruth! We'll ask him if he could hit eighty home runs in one year.

Carla: Great idea! I've heard of your time-travel machine. Now I'm going to ride in it!

Tommy: All I have to do is set the date and place, push this button, and ... we're back in Yankee Stadium in March 1927.

Tammy: There's Babe Ruth taking batting practice. There goes another one over the wall! I can't believe Babe Ruth is doing so well. He looks like he's out of shape.

Carla: Watch him run around the bases! He's breathing hard.

Babe Ruth: Whew! After all that hitting and running, I'm hungry.

Tammy: Babe is eating four hot dogs! Doesn't he know it's not healthy to pig out on foods that are high in fat?

Lou Gehrig: The Babe eats anything he wants, anytime he wants.

Tommy: You're Lou Gehrig, Babe's teammate!

Carla: Don't you players lift weights and work out?

Lou: Not much. We just go out and play ball.

Tommy: You don't exercise and train?

Babe: Exercise? I'd rather go to parties and stay up late . . . (he yawns) even though I am tired today.

Tommy: Babe, some people say you're the best player ever. Other people think Terry Fox is better. He's going to try to hit eighty home runs this season.

Babe: Eighty home runs! That's impossible.

Carla: He eats right and exercises every day.

Tommy: I wonder how many home runs you'd hit, Babe, if you were in better shape.

Tammy: And got enough sleep.

Lou: More than Terry Fox.

Babe: You think so?

Lou: If you were in better shape, you'd run faster.

Tammy: Come with us, Babe, and we'll find out how good you really are.

Tommy: We'll explain everything on the way. Just step into the *When Machine.* I push this button and ... here we are back in the present.

Tammy: We're at the spring training camp for Terry Fox's team, the Metros.

Tommy: And that's the manager, Joe Van Horn.

Joe Van Horn: Hi, kids. Want to watch?

Carla: Look, there's Terry!

Terry Fox: Hi, kids. Who is your friend? He looks familiar.

Tommy: This is Babe Ruth. He came to play with Terry Fox.

Terry: Babe Ruth! What an honor to meet you.

Babe: I've heard a lot of good things about you, too.

Terry: Let's talk about hitting while we run laps around the field.

Babe: Run laps? Why?

Terry: You have to be in good shape to play great baseball.

Babe: Just give me a bat and I'll show you great baseball.

Joe: Okay, Babe, you're up.

Tammy: Here's the pitch.

Tommy: Babe hit the ball hard! It's a triple for sure.

Carla: I don't know. Look at Babe huffing and puffing around the bases.

Tammy: He's sliding into third . . . Luis Garcia tagged Babe out!

Luis Garcia: You have to run faster than that if you want to play with us.

Babe: Whew! After all that running, I need a bottle of soda-pop.

Luis: Soda-pop? That's full of sugar. You don't want to drink that.

Terry: Water is really good for your body, especially when you're exercising.

Joe: Okay, everyone, that's it for today. Don't eat too much. And go to bed early.

Babe: Is he serious about eating a light dinner and going to bed early?

Terry: Of course. Eating good foods and getting enough sleep help keep our bodies strong and healthy.

Luis: You can't be a good athlete if you stuff your body with junk.

Tommy: He's right, Babe. These players are in super shape. You'll have to take care of your body if you hope to hit as many homers as Terry!

Terry: I'll treat everyone to dinner. We'll show Babe which foods are healthy.

Luis: Foods like vegetables, fruits, whole grains, and lean meats.

Babe: I can't promise I'll like those foods, but I'll try them.

Tommy: That's a winning attitude, Babe.

Babe: Terry is a smart ballplayer. Maybe I can pick up a few tips from him.

Terry: Me giving tips to Babe Ruth! Wow!

Babe: I think I'll stick around for a few weeks.

A few weeks later . . .

Luis: Go, Babe! What a catch! I never thought he'd reach that fly ball.

Joe: Babe has been working hard.

Terry: He works out at the gym with me every day.

Tommy: He's been eating lots of nutritious foods, too!

Carla: And going to bed early.

Babe: I ran as fast as I could to catch that ball, but I'm not out of breath. I can't believe how good I feel. Let's bust some baseballs!

Johnny Sula: Are you ready for my pitches?

Babe: The way I feel, I can hit anything!

Johnny: Then try this!

Tammy: Here comes the pitch. Babe swings! Smack!

Carla: I love that sound.

Johnny: I hate that sound. Look at the ball go!

Tommy: It's going, going—

Carla: A home run!

Johnny: I've never seen anyone hit a pitch so far!

Tommy: Not even Terry Fox?

Johnny: Not even Terry Fox.

Joe: It's been great having you in spring training, Babe. Will you play for us?

Terry: Now that you're exercising and eating right, maybe we'll both hit eighty home runs!

Johnny: Say yes, Babe! If you're on my team, I'll never have to pitch to you again!

Babe: I'd love to play with you guys, but my Yankee teammates need me. Now that I'm in shape, I'll be able to smash more home runs!

Tommy: Good luck, Babe. I know you'll do great!

Babe: Thanks for showing me how important it is to eat right, exercise, and take care of my body.

Tommy: Step into the *When Machine* . . . and back you go to the Yankees.

Babe: Bye, everyone!

Carla: So how did Babe do that year?

Tommy: In 1927, Babe hit sixty home runs.

Tammy: No one broke that record for more than thirty years.

Tommy: Babe ended up hitting 714 home runs in his career.

Tammy: That was a record for almost forty years.

Tommy: So, Carla, do you agree that Babe Ruth is the greatest player ever?

Carla: Babe was the greatest then. Terry Fox is the greatest now. But the greatest ever? I'd say that with all that I've learned about physical fitness and nutritious eating, the record books better make room for . . . me!

The End